#858
51

Bod's Apple

MICHAEL and JOANNE COLE

Follett Publishing Company

Chicago New York

Library of Congress Catalog Card Number: AC 66-10000

First Printing

Follett Publishing Company
1010 West Washington Boulevard
Chicago, Illinois 60607

T/L 0805

Here is Bod holding an apple. "I'm going to throw this apple up in the air and catch it," he says. "Watch me!"

He throws the apple up in the air—and waits for
it to come down.

But it doesn't come down.
"That's funny," says Bod.

Just then his Aunt Flo comes along. "Hello, Bod,"
says Aunt Flo. "What are you doing here?"
"I'm waiting for an apple I threw up in the air,"

says Bod. "It hasn't come down."
"It will," says Aunt Flo. "They always do." And
she waits with Bod for the apple to come down.

Then along comes Frank the postman with a letter
for Aunt Flo. "Hello," says Frank. "Why are you
standing here?"
"We're waiting for an apple that Bod threw up in

the air to come down again," says Aunt Flo. "Can
you see it?"
"No," says Frank. "But it's sure to come down
soon. I'll wait with you and Bod."

A little later Farmer Barleymow comes by. "Hello," he says. "What's going on?"
"We're waiting for Bod's apple," says Frank. "He threw it up in the air and it hasn't come down yet."

"It'll be down," says Farmer Barleymow. "What goes up must come down."
And Farmer Barleymow waits with Frank, Aunt Flo, and Bod for the apple to come down.

The next person to come along is Officer Bobby.
"Hello, hello," says Officer Bobby. "What are you
all waiting here for?"
"An apple," says Farmer Barleymow.

"An APPLE?" says Officer Bobby.
"Yes, an apple," says Farmer Barleymow. "Bod
threw it up in the air, and we're still waiting for it
to come down."

13

"Then you must be daft!" says Officer Bobby. "How can an apple stay up in the air so long? It must have been stolen by a bird. Now, move along there!"

14

Farmer Barleymow feels very foolish and goes red in the face. "I must be daft," he thinks, "wasting my time here when I could be driving my tractor."

He turns to Frank the postman and says, "You must be daft, Frank, waiting here. How can the apple still be up in the air?"

Now Frank feels very foolish and goes red in the face. "I must be daft," he thinks, "wasting my time here when I could be taking around letters."

He turns to Aunt Flo and says, "Excuse me, madam, but you must be daft waiting here. How can the apple still be up in the air?"

Now Aunt Flo feels very foolish and goes red in the face. "I must be daft," thinks Aunt Flo, "wasting my time here when I could be baking a cake."

And she turns to Bod and says, "You must be daft! How can the apple still be up in the air after all this time? Honestly, Bod, sometimes I think you need your bumps felt."

Now it is Bod's turn to feel foolish and go red in the face. "I must be daft," he thinks, "waiting around here when I could be getting another apple to throw up in the air and catch."

And he is just going to walk away when . . .

BONK! The apple comes down on his head and knocks him flat.

When they hear the BONK, Officer Bobby, Farmer Barleymow, Frank the postman, and Aunt Flo all turn around. They are amazed at what they see.

Bod has a bump on his head the size of an apple,
and an apple at his feet the size of the bump.

But he is so glad to get his apple back that he doesn't mind the bump. In fact, he's rather proud of it.

"You said I needed my bumps felt," he says to
Aunt Flo. "Come and feel this one."

Then Officer Bobby, Farmer Barleymow, Frank,
and Aunt Flo all buy apples

and throw them in the air to see how long they will stay up.

But

their apples come straight down again.

Why did Bod's apple stay up so long?
Do you know?